RUMER GODDEN

The Story of Holly & Ivy

Illustrated by
Christian Birmingham

MACMILLAN CHILDREN'S BOOKS

First published in 1958

This edition published 2005 by Macmillan Children's Books
a division of Macmillan Publishers Limited
20 New Wharf Road, London N1 9RR
Basingstoke and Oxford
www.panmacmillan.com

Associated companies throughout the world.

ISBN 0 330 43974 X

1 3 5 7 9 8 6 4 2

A CIP catalogue record for this book is available from
the British Library.

Typeset by Intype Libra Ltd
Printed and bound in Great Britain by
Mackays of Chatham plc, Chatham, Kent

This is a story about wishing. It is also about a doll and a little girl. It begins with the doll.

Her name, of course, was Holly.

It could not have been anything else, for she was dressed for Christmas in a red dress, and red shoes, though her petticoat and socks were green.

She was ten inches high and carefully jointed; she had real gold hair, brown glass eyes, and teeth like tiny china pearls.

It was the morning of Christmas Eve, the last day before Christmas. The toys in Mr Blossom's toyshop in the little country town stirred and shook themselves after the long night. 'We must be sold today,' they said.

'Today?' asked Holly. She had been unpacked only the day before and was the newest toy in the shop.

Outside in the street it was snowing, but the

toyshop window was lit and warm – it had been lit all night. The spinning tops showed their glinting colours, the balls their bands of red and yellow and blue; the trains were ready to run round and round. There were steamboats and electric boats; the sailing boats shook out their fresh white sails. The clockwork toys had each its private key; the tea sets gleamed in their boxes. There were aeroplanes, trumpets, and doll perambulators; the rocking horses looked as if they were prancing, and the teddy bears held up their furry arms. There was every kind of stuffed animal – rabbits and lions and tigers, dogs and cats, even turtles with real shells. The dolls were on a long glass shelf decorated with tinsel – baby dolls and bride dolls, with bridesmaids in every colour, a boy doll in a kilt

and another who was a sailor. One girl doll was holding her gloves, another had an umbrella. They were all beautiful, but none of them had been sold.

'We must be sold today,' said the dolls.

'Today,' said Holly.

Like the teddy bears, the dolls held out their arms. Toys, of course, think the opposite way to you. 'We shall have a little boy or girl for Christmas,' said the toys.

'Will I?' asked Holly.

'We shall have homes.'

'Will I?' asked Holly.

The toys knew what homes were like from the broken dolls who came to the shop to be mended.

'There are warm fires and lights,' said the dolls, 'rooms filled with lovely things. We feel children's hands.'

'Bah! Children's hands are rough,' said the big toy

owl who sat on a pretend branch below the dolls. 'They are rough. They can squeeze.'

'I want to be squeezed,' said a little elephant.

'We have never felt a child's hands,' said two baby hippopotamuses. They were made of grey velvet, and their pink velvet mouths were open and as wide as the rest of them. Their names were Mallow and Wallow. 'We have never felt a child's hands.'

Neither, of course, had Holly.

The owl's name was Abracadabra. He was so big and important that he thought the toyshop belonged to him.

'I thought it belonged to Mr Blossom,' said Holly.

'Hsst! T-whoo!' said Abracadabra, which was his way of being cross. 'Does a new little doll dare to speak?'

'Be careful. Be careful,' the dolls warned Holly.

Abracadabra had widespread wings marked with yellow and brown, a big hooked beak, and white felt feet like claws. Above his eyes were two fierce black tufts, and the eyes themselves were so big and green that they made green shadows on his round white cheeks. His eyes saw everything, even at night. Even the biggest toys were afraid of Abracadabra. Mallow and Wallow shook on their round stubby feet each time he spoke.

'He might think we're mice,' said Mallow and Wallow.

'My mice,' said Abracadabra.

'Mr Blossom's mice,' said Holly.

Holly's place on the glass shelf was quite close to Abracadabra. He gave her a look with his green eyes. 'This is the last day for shopping,' said Abracadabra. 'Tomorrow the shop will be shut.'

A shiver went round all the dolls, but Holly knew Abracadabra was talking to her.

'But the fathers and mothers will come today,' said the little elephant. He was called Crumple because his skin did not fit but hung in comfortable folds round his neck and his knees. He had a scarlet flannel saddle hung with bells, and his trunk, his mouth, and his tail all turned up, which gave him a cheerful expression. It was easy for Crumple to be cheerful; on his saddle was a ticket marked 'Sold'. He had only to be made into a parcel.

'Will I be a parcel?' asked Holly.

'I am sure you will,' said Crumple, and he waved his trunk at her and told the dolls, 'You will be put into Christmas stockings.'

'Oooh!' said the dolls longingly.

'Or hung on Christmas trees.'

'Aaaah!' said the dolls.

'But you won't all be sold,' said Abracadabra, and Holly knew he was talking to her.

The sound of the key in the lock was heard. It was Mr Blossom come to open the shop. Peter the shop boy was close behind him. 'We shall be busy today,' said Mr Blossom.

'Yes-sir,' said Peter.

There could be no more talking, but, 'We can wish. We must wish,' whispered the dolls, and Holly whispered, 'I am wishing.'

'Hoo! Hoo!' went Abracadabra. It did not matter if Peter and Mr Blossom heard him; it was his toy-owl sound. 'Hoo! Hoo!' They did not know but the toys all knew that it was Abracadabra's way of laughing.

The toys thought that all children have homes, but all children have not.

Far away in the city was a big house called St Agnes's, where thirty boys and girls had to live together, but now, for three days, they were saying 'Goodbye' to St Agnes's. 'A kind lady – or gentleman – has asked you for Christmas,' Miss Shepherd, who looked after them all, had told them, and one by one the children were called for or taken to the train. Soon there would be no one left in the big house but Miss Shepherd and Ivy.

Ivy was a little girl, six years old with

straight hair cut in a fringe, blue-grey eyes, and a turned-up nose. She had a green coat the colour of her name, and red gloves, but no lady or gentleman had asked for her for Christmas. 'I don't care,' said Ivy.

Sometimes in Ivy there was an empty feeling, and the emptiness ached; it ached so much that she had to say something quickly in case she cried, and, 'I don't care at all,' said Ivy.

'You will care,' said the last boy, Barnabas, who was waiting for a taxi. 'Cook has gone, the maids have gone, and Miss Shepherd is going to her sister. You will care,' said Barnabas.

'I won't,' said Ivy, and she said more quickly, 'I'm going to my grandmother.'

'You haven't got a grandmother,' said Barnabas. 'We don't have them.' That was true. The boys and girls at St Agnes's had no fathers and mothers, let alone grandmothers.

'But I have,' said Ivy. 'At Appleton.'

I do not know how that name came into Ivy's head. Perhaps she had heard it somewhere. She said it again. 'In Appleton.'

'Bet you haven't,' said Barnabas, and he went on saying that until his taxi came.

11

When Barnabas had gone Miss Shepherd said, 'Ivy, I shall have to send you to the country, to our Infants' Home.'

'Infants are babies,' said Ivy. 'I'm not a baby.'

But Miss Shepherd only said, 'There is nowhere else for you to go.'

'I'll go to my grandmother,' said Ivy.

'You haven't got a grandmother,' said Miss Shepherd. 'I'm sorry to send you to the Infants' Home, for there won't be much for you to see there or anyone to talk to, but I don't know what else to do with you. My sister has influenza and I have to go and nurse her.'

'I'll help you,' said Ivy.

'You might catch it,' said Miss Shepherd. 'That wouldn't do.' And she took Ivy to the station and put her on the train.

She put Ivy's suitcase in the rack and gave her a packet of sandwiches, an apple, a ticket, two shillings, and a parcel that was her Christmas present; on to Ivy's coat she pinned a label with the address of the Infant's Home. 'Be a good girl,' said Miss Shepherd.

When Miss Shepherd had gone Ivy tore the label off and threw it out of the window. 'I'm going

to my grandmother,' said Ivy.

All day long people came in and out of the toyshop. Mr Blossom and Peter were so busy they could hardly snatch a cup of tea.

Crumple was made into a parcel and taken away; teddy bears and sailing ships were brought out of the window; dolls were lifted down from the shelf. The boy doll in the kilt and the doll with gloves were sold, and baby dolls and brides.

Holly held out her arms and smiled her

china smile. Each time a little girl came to the window and looked, pressing her face against the glass, Holly asked, 'Are you my Christmas girl?' Each time the shop door opened she was sure it was for her.

'I am here. I am Holly'; and she wished, 'Ask for me. Lift me down. Ask!' But nobody asked.

'Hoo! Hoo!' said Abracadabra.

Ivy was still in the train. She had eaten her sandwiches almost at once and opened her present. She had hoped and believed she would have a doll this Christmas, but the present was a pencil box. A doll would have filled up the emptiness – and now it ached so much that Ivy had to press her lips together tightly, and, 'My grandmother will give me a doll,' she said out loud.

'Will she, dear?' asked a lady sitting opposite, and the people in the carriage all looked at Ivy and smiled. 'And where does your grandmother live?' asked a gentleman.

'In Appleton,' said Ivy.

The lady nodded. 'That will be two or three stations,' she said.

Then . . . there is an Appleton, thought Ivy.

The lady got out, more people got in, and the train went on. Ivy grew sleepy watching the snowflakes fly past the window. The train seemed to be going very fast, and she leaned her head against the carriage cushions and shut her eyes. When she opened them the train had stopped at a small station and the people in her carriage were all getting out. The gentleman lifted her suitcase down from the rack. 'A . p . . t . n,' said the notice boards. Ivy could not read very well but she knew A was for 'Appleton'.

Forgetting all about her suitcase and the pencil box, she jumped down from the train, slammed the carriage door behind her, and followed the crowd of people as they went through the station gate. The ticket collector had so many tickets he did not look at hers; in a moment Ivy was out in the street, and the train chuffed out of the station. 'I don't care,' said Ivy. 'This is where my grandmother lives.'

The country town looked pleasant and clean after the city. There were cobbled streets going up and down, and houses with gables overhanging the pavements and roofs jumbled together. Some of the houses had windows with many small panes; some had doors with brass knockers. The paint was bright and the curtains clean. 'I like where my grandmother lives,' said Ivy.

Presently she came to the market square where the Christmas market was going on. There were stalls of turkeys and geese, fruit stalls with oranges, apples, nuts, and tangerines that are like small oranges wrapped in silver paper. Some stalls had holly, mistletoe, and Christmas trees, some had flowers; there were stalls of china and glass and one with wooden spoons and bowls. A woman was selling balloons and an old man was cooking hot chestnuts. Men were shouting, the women had shopping bags and baskets, the children were running, everyone was buying or selling and laughing. Ivy had spent all her life in St Agnes's; she had not seen a market before; and, 'I won't look for my grandmother yet,' said Ivy.

In the toyshop Mr Blossom had never made so much money, Peter had never worked so hard. Peter was fifteen; he had red cheeks and a smile as wide as Mallow's and Wallow's; he took good care of the toys and did everything he could to help Mr Blossom. Whish! went the brown paper as Peter pulled it off the roll, whirr! went the string ball, snip-snap, the scissors cut off the string. He did up dozens of parcels, ran up and down the stepladder, fetched and carried and took away. 'That abominable boy will sell every toy in the shop,' grumbled Abracadabra.

'What's abominable?' asked Holly.

'It means not good,' said dolls, 'but he is good. Dear, dear Peter!' whispered the dolls, but Abracadabra's green eyes had caught the light from a passing car. They gave a flash and, rattle-bang! Peter fell down the stepladder from top to bottom. He bumped his elbow, grazed his knee, and tore a big hole in his pocket. 'Hold

on! Go slow!' said
Mr Blossom.

'Yes-sir,' said
poor Peter in a
very little voice.

'Did you see
that, did you see
that?' whispered
the dolls. Holly
wished she were
farther away
from Abracadabra.

Soon all the baby dolls but one were sold
and most of the teddy bears. Mallow and
Wallow were taken for twin boys' stockings;
they were done up in two little parcels and
carried away. Hardly a ball was left, and not a
single aeroplane. The sailor doll was sold, and
the doll with the umbrella, but still no one had
asked for Holly.

Dolls are not like us; we are alive as soon as
we are born, but dolls are not really alive until
they are played with. 'I want to be played with,'
said Holly, 'I want someone to move my arms
and legs, to make me open and shut my eyes. I

wish! I wish!' said Holly.

It began to be dark. The dusk made the lighted window shine so brightly that everyone stopped to look in. The children pressed their faces so closely against the glass that the tips of noses looked like white cherries. Holly held out her arms and smiled her china smile, but the children walked away. 'Stop. Stop,' wished Holly, but they did not stop.

Abracadabra's eyes shone in the dusk. Holly began to be very much afraid.

One person stopped, but it was not a boy or a girl. It was Mrs Jones, the policeman's wife from down the street. She was passing the toyshop on her way home when Holly's red dress caught her eye. 'Pretty!' said Mrs Jones and stopped.

You and I would have felt Holly's wish at once, but

Mrs Jones had no children and it was so long since she had known a doll that she did not understand; only a feeling stirred in her that she had not had for a long time, a feeling of Christmas, and when she got home she told Mr Jones, 'This year we shall have a tree.'

'Don't be daft,' said Mr Jones, but when Mrs Jones had put her shopping away, a chicken and a small plum-pudding for her and Mr Jones's Christmas dinner, a piece of fish for the cat, and a dozen fine handkerchiefs which were Mr Jones's present, she went back to the market and bought some holly, mistletoe, and a Christmas tree.

'A tree with tinsel,' said Mrs Jones. She bought some tinsel. 'And candles,' she said.

'Candles are prettier than electric light.' She brought twelve red candles. 'They need candle clips,' she said, and bought twelve of those. And a tree should have

some balls, thought Mrs Jones, glass balls in jewel colours, ruby-red, emerald-green, and gold. She bought some balls and a box of tiny silver crackers and a tinsel star. When she got home she stood the tree in the window and dressed it, putting the star on the top.

'Who is to look at it?' asked Mr Jones.

Mrs Jones thought for a moment and said, 'Christmas needs children, Albert.' Albert was Mr Jones's name. 'I wonder,' said Mrs Jones. 'Couldn't we find a little girl?'

'What's the matter with you today, my dear?' said Mr Jones. 'How could we find a little girl? You're daft.' And it was a little sadly that Mrs Jones put holly along the chimney shelf, hung mistletoe in the hall, tied a bunch of holly on the doorknocker, and went back to her housework.

Ivy was happy in the market. She walked round and round the stalls, looking at all the things; sometimes a snowflake fell on her head but she shook it off; sometimes one stuck to her cheek, but she put out her tongue and licked it away. She bought a bag of chestnuts from the chestnut man; they were hot in her hands and she ate them one by one. She had a cup of tea from a tea stall on wheels, and from a sweet stall she bought a toffee apple. When her legs grew tired she sat down on a step and wrapped the ends of her coat round her knees. When she was cold she started to walk again.

Soon lights were lit all along the stalls; they looked like stars. The crowd grew thicker. People laughed and stamped in the snow to keep their feet warm; Ivy stamped too. The stall-keepers shouted and called for people to come and buy. Ivy bought a blue balloon.

At St Agnes's a telegraph boy rang the bell. He had a telegram for Miss Shepherd from the Infants' Home. It said, IVY NOT ARRIVED. SUPPOSE SHE IS WITH YOU. MERRY CHRISTMAS.

The boy rang and rang, but there was no one at St Agnes's to answer the bell, and at last he put a notice in the letterbox, got on his bicycle, and rode away.

In her house down the street Mrs Jones kept looking at the Christmas tree. 'Oughtn't there

to be presents?' she asked. It was so long since she had had a tree of her own that she could not be sure. She took Mr Jones's handkerchiefs, wrapped them in white paper and tied them with some red ribbon she had by her, and put the parcel at the foot of the tree. That looked better but still not quite right.

'There ought to be toys,' said Mrs Jones, and she called to Mr Jones, 'Albert!'

Mr Jones looked up from the newspaper he was reading.

'Would it be very silly, Albert?' asked Mrs Jones.

'Would what be silly?'

'Would it be silly to buy . . . a little doll?'

'What is the matter with you today?' asked Mr Jones, and he said again, 'You're daft.'

Soon it was time for him to go on duty.

'I shall be out all night,' he told Mrs Jones.

'Two of the men are away

sick. I shall take a short sleep at the police station and go on duty again. See you in the morning,' said Mr Jones.

He kissed Mrs Jones goodbye and went out, but put his head round the door again. 'Have a good breakfast waiting for me,' said Mr Jones.

In the toyshop it was closing time.

'What does that mean?' asked Holly.

'That it's over,' said Abracadabra.

'Over?' Holly did not understand.

Mr Blossom pulled the blind down on the door and put up a notice: 'Closed'.

'Closed. Hoo! Hoo!' said Abracadabra.

Mr Blossom was so tired he told Peter to tidy the shop. 'And you can lock up. Can I trust you?' asked Mr Blossom.

'Yes-sir,' said Peter.

'Be careful of the key,' said Mr Blossom.

'Yes-sir,' said Peter proudly. It was the first time Mr Blossom had trusted him with the key.

'You have been a good boy,' said Mr Blossom as he was going. 'You may choose any toy you like – except the expensive ones like air guns or electric trains. Yes, choose yourself a toy,' said Mr Blossom. 'Good night.'

When Mr Blossom had gone; 'A toy!' said Peter, and he asked, 'What does he think I am? A blooming kid?'

Peter swept up the bits of paper and string and straw and put them in the rubbish bin at the back of the shop. He was so tired he forgot to put the lid on the bin. Then he dusted the counter, but he was too tired to do any more, so he put on his overcoat to go home. He turned out the lights – it was no use lighting the window now that the shopping was over – stepped outside, and closed and locked the door. If he had waited a moment he would have heard a stirring, a noise, tiny whimperings. 'What about us? What about us?' It was the toys.

'Go home and good riddance!' said Abracadabra to Peter; but the toys cried, 'Don't go! Don't go!'

Peter heard nothing. He put the key in his jacket pocket to keep it quite safe and turned to run home.

The key fell straight through the torn pocket into the snow. It did not make a sound.

'Hoo! Hoo!' said Abracadabra, and the snowflakes began to cover the key as Peter ran off.

The market was over as well. The crowd had gone, the stalls were packing up, the last Christmas trees were being sold. Ivy had spent all her money, the blue balloon had burst, her legs ached with tiredness, and she shivered.

Then the lights went out; there were only pools of yellow from the lamp posts, with patches of darkness between. A bit of paper blew against Ivy's legs, making her jump. Suddenly the market place seemed large and strange; she would have liked to see Miss Shepherd.

You might think that Ivy cried, but she was not that kind of little girl. Though the empty feeling ached inside her she pressed her lips tightly together, then said, 'It's time I looked for my grandmother,' and started off to look.

*

She walked up the cobbled streets between the houses.

How cosy they seemed, with their lighted windows; smoke was going up from every chimney. 'There are fires and beds and supper,' said Ivy. Some of the houses had wreaths of holly on their front doors, paper chains and garlands in their rooms; and in almost every window was a Christmas tree.

When Ivy looked in she could see children. In one house they were sitting round a table, eating; in another they were hanging stockings from the chimney shelf; in some they were doing up parcels, but, 'I must look for a house

with a tree and no children,' said Ivy.

She knew there would be a tree, 'Because my grandmother is expecting me,' said Ivy.

The toyshop was still and dark. 'Thank goodness!' said Abracadabra.

'But people can't see us,' said Holly.

'Why should they see us?' asked Abracadabra. 'It's over. People have all gone home. The children are going to bed.' He sounded pleased. 'There will be no more shopping,' said Abracadabra, and the whisper rang round the toys, 'No shopping. No shopping.'

'Then . . . we are the ones not sold,' said a doll.

There was a long silence.

'I can be sold any time,' said a bride doll at last. 'Weddings are always.'

'I am in yellow, with primroses,' said a bridesmaid. 'I shall be sold in the spring.'

'I am in pink, with roses,' said another. 'They will buy me in the summer.'

But Holly had a red dress, for Christmas. What would be done with her?

'You will be put back into stock,' said Abracadabra.

'Please . . . what is stock?' whispered Holly.

'It is shut up and dark,' said Abracadabra, as if he liked that very much. 'No one sees you or disturbs you. You get covered with dust, and I shall be there,' said Abracadabra.

Holly wished she could crack.

'This is my grandmother's house,' said Ivy, but when she got to the house it was not. That happened several times. 'Then it's that one,' she said, but it was not that one either. She began to be very cold and tired.

Somebody came down the street. Even in the snow his tread was loud. It was a big policeman. (As a matter of fact, it was Mr Jones.)

Ivy knew as well as you or I know that policemen are kind people and do not like little girls to wander about alone after dark in a strange town. 'He might send me to the Infants' Home,' said Ivy and, quick as a mouse going into its hole, she whisked into a passage between two shops.

'Queer!' said Mr Jones. 'I thought I saw something green.'

At the end of the passage was a shed, and Ivy whisked into it and stood behind the door. There was something odd about that shed – it was warm. Ivy did not know how an empty shed could be warm on a cold night, but I shall tell you.

The shed belonged to a baker and was built against the wall behind his oven. All day he had been baking bread and rolls for Christmas, and the oven was still hot. When Ivy put her hand on the wall she had to take it away quickly, for the wall was baking hot.

Soon she stopped shivering. In a corner was a pile of flour sacks, and she sat down on them.

A lamp in the passageway outside gave just enough light. Ivy's legs began to feel heavy and warm; her fingers and toes seem to uncurl and stretch in the warmth, while her eyelids seemed to curl up. She gave a great yawn.

Then she took off her coat, lay down on the sacks, and spread the coat over her.

In a moment she was fast asleep.

The toyshop was close by the passage. It was too dark to be noticed, though Abracadabra's eyes shone like green lamps.

'Shopping is over. Hoo! Hoo!' said Abracadabra.

'Over. Over,' mourned the toys.

They did not know and Abracadabra did not know that it is when shopping is over that Christmas begins.

Soon it was not dark, for the snow had stopped and the moon came up and lighted all the town. The roofs sparkled with frost as did the snow on the pavements and roads. In the toyshop window the toys showed, not as bright as day, but bright as moonlight, which is far more beautiful. Holly's dress looked a pale red, and her hair was pale gold.

Dolls do not lie down to go to sleep; they only do that when you remember to put them to bed and, as you often forget, they would be tired if they had to wait; they can sleep where they stand or sit, and now the dolls in the toyshop window slept in their places, all but Holly. She could not go to sleep. She was a Christmas doll and it was beginning to be Christmas. She could not know why, but she was excited. Then all at once, softly, bells began to ring.

Long after most children are in bed, on Christmas Eve, the church bells in towns and villages begin to ring. Soon the clocks strike twelve and it is Christmas.

Holly heard the bells and – what was this? People were walking in the street – hurrying.

'Hsst! T-whoo!' said Abracadabra at them as they passed, but they took no notice.

'Then . . . it has started,' said Holly.

'What has started?' said Abracadabra.

'It,' said Holly. She could not explain better than that for she did not know yet what 'it' meant – this was, after all, her first Christmas – but the bells grew louder and more and more people passed. Then, it may have been the pin of Holly's price ticket, or a spine of tinsel come loose from the shelf, but Holly felt a tiny pricking as sharp as a prickle on a holly leaf. 'Wish,' said the prickle. 'Wish.'

'But – the shop is closed,' said Holly. 'The children are in bed. Abracadabra says I must go into sto –' The prickle interrupted. 'Wish. Wish!' said the prickle. 'Wish!' It went on till Holly wished.

Ivy thought the bells woke her or perhaps the passing feet, but then why did she feel something sharp like a thistle or a hard straw in one of the sacks? She sat up, but she was half-asleep and she thought the feet were the St Agnes's children marching down to breakfast and the bells were the breakfast bell. Then she saw she was still in the shed, though it was filled with a new light, a strange silver light. 'Moonlight?' asked Ivy and rubbed her eyes. She was warm and comfortable on the sacks under the green coat – though there were great white patches on it from the flour – too warm and comfortable to move, and she lay down, but again she felt that thistle or sharp straw. The light seemed to be calling her, the bells, the hurrying feet; the prickle seemed to tell her to get up.

Ivy put on her coat and went out.

Outside in the passage the footsteps sounded so loud that she guessed it was the policeman. She waited until they had passed before she dared come out.

In the street the moonlight was so bright that once again Ivy thought it was morning and she was in St Agnes's and the bells were the breakfast bell. 'Only . . . there are so many of them,' said sleepy Ivy.

She walked a few steps to the toyshop. She did not know how it came to be there and she thought she was in her St Agnes's bedroom and it was filled with toys. Then: 'Not toys,' said Ivy, 'a toy,' and she was wide-awake. She did not even see Abracadabra glaring at her with his green eyes; she looked straight at Holly.

She saw Holly's dress and socks and shoes. She is red and green too, thought Ivy. She saw Holly's hair, brown eyes, little teeth, and beautiful joints. They were just what Ivy liked and, 'My Christmas doll!' said Ivy.

Holly saw Ivy's face pressed against the window as she had seen so many children's faces that day, but, 'This one is different,' said Holly.

Ivy's hands in their woollen gloves held to the ledge where it said, BLOSSOM, HIGH-CLASS TOYS AND GAMES. Holly looked at Ivy's hands. Soon they will be holding me, thought Holly. Ivy's coat even in the moonlight was as beautiful a green as Holly's dress was a beautiful red, so that they seemed to match, and, 'My Christmas girl!' said Holly.

Ivy had to go to the shed again to get warm, but I cannot tell you how many times she came back to look at Holly.

'My Christmas doll!'

'My Christmas girl!'

'But the window is in between,' said Abracadabra.

The window was in between and the toyshop door was locked, but even if it had been open Ivy had no money. 'Hoo! Hoo!' said Abracadabra, but, remember, not only Holly but Ivy was wishing now.

'I wish . . .'

'I wish . . .'

The toys woke up. 'A child,' they whispered, 'a child.' And they wished too.

Wishes are powerful things. Ivy stepped

back from the window and Abracadabra's eyes grew pale as, cr-runch went something under Ivy's heel. It was something hidden just under the snow.

'Hisst!' said Abracadabra. 'T-whoo!' But Ivy bent down and picked up a key.

In the moonlight it was bright silver. 'Peter's key. Peter's key,' whispered the toys.

Footsteps sounded in the street, people were coming from church; Ivy put the key in her pocket and quickly ran back to the shed.

She had to wait a long time for the people to pass as they stopped to say 'Merry Christmas' to one another, to give each other parcels; and Ivy sat down on the sacks to rest. Presently she gave another great yawn. Presently she lay down and spread her coat over her. Presently she went to sleep.

The toys had gone to sleep too. 'But I can't,' said Holly. 'I must wait for my Christmas girl.'

She stayed awake for a long time, but she was only a little doll . . . and presently she fell asleep where she stood.

Ivy dreamed that the shed was hung with holly wreaths and lit with candles. The berries were the colour of the Christmas doll's dress and the candle flames were as bright as her hair. 'A-aaah!' said Ivy.

Holly dreamed that two arms were cradling her, that hands were holding her, that her dress was beginning to be rumpled and her eyes made to open and shut. 'A-aaah!' said Holly.

Abracadabra kept his green eyes wide open, but he could not stop the moon from going down, nor the coming of Christmas Day.

*

Very early on Christmas morning Mrs Jones got up and tidied her living room. She lit a fire, swept the hearth, and dusted the furniture. She laid a table for breakfast with a pink and white cloth, her best blue china, a loaf of crusty bread, a pat of new butter in a glass dish, honey in a blue pot, a bowl of sugar, and a jug of milk. She had some fresh brown eggs and, in the kitchen, she put sausages to sizzle in a pan. Then she set the teapot to warm on the hob, lighted the candles on the Christmas tree, and sat down by the fire to wait.

The baker's oven cooled in the night and Ivy woke with the cold. The shed was icy; Ivy's eyelashes were stuck together with rime, and the tip of her nose felt frozen. When she tried to stand up, her legs were so stiff that she almost fell over; when she put on her coat her fingers were so numb that they could not do up the buttons. Ivy was a sensible little girl; she knew she had to get warm and she did not cry, but, 'I m-must h-hop and sk-skip,' she said through her chattering teeth, and there in the shed she swung her arms, in-out, out-in, and clapped her

42

hands. Outside she tried to run, but her legs felt heavy and her head seemed to swim. 'I m-must f-find m-my g-g-grandmother qu-qu-quickly,' said Ivy.

She went into the street, and how cold it was there! The wind blew under her coat; the snow on the pavements had turned to ice and was slippery. She tried to hop, but the snow was like glass. Ivy fingers and nose hurt in the cold. 'If-f I l-look at m-my d-d-doll, I m-might-t f-feel b-b-b-better,' said Ivy, but she turned the wrong way.

It was the wrong way for the toyshop, but perhaps it was the right way for Ivy, for a hundred yards down the street she came to the Jones's' house.

I must look for a house with a tree and no children. That is what she had said. Now she looked in at the window and there was no sign of any children but there was a Christmas tree lit. Ivy saw the fire – 'To w-warm m-me,' whispered Ivy, and, oh, she was cold! She saw the table with the pink and white cloth, blue china, bread and butter, honey and milk, the teapot warming – 'My b-breakfast,' whispered Ivy

and, oh, she was hungry! She saw Mrs Jones sitting by the fire, in her clean apron, waiting. Ivy stood quite still. Then: 'My g-g-grandmother,' whispered Ivy.

Holly woke with a start. 'Oh! I have been asleep,' said Holly in dismay. 'Oh! I must have missed my little Christmas girl.'

'She won't be back,' said Abracadabra. 'It's Christmas Day. She's playing with her new toys.'

'I am her new toy,' said Holly.

'Hoo! Hoo!' said Abracadabra.

'I am,' said Holly, and she wished. I think

her wish was bigger than Abracadabra, for when Ivy lifted her hand to Mrs Jones's knocker, a prickle from the bunch of holly ran into her finger. 'Ow!' said Ivy. The prickle was so sharp that she took her hand down, and 'F-first I must g-get my d-d-doll,' said Ivy.

If Ivy had stopped to think she would have known she could not get her doll. How could she when the shop was locked and the window was in between? Besides, Holly was not Ivy's doll and had not even been sold. A wise person would have known this, but sometimes it is better to feel a prickle than to be wise.

'Hullo,' said Ivy to Holly through the toyshop window. 'G-g-good morning.'

Holly could not say 'Hullo' back, but she could wish Ivy good morning – with a doll's wish.

In the daylight Holly was even more beautiful than she had been by moonlight, Ivy was even dearer.

'A little girl!' sneered

45

Abracadabra. 'There are hundreds of little girls.'

'Not for me,' said Holly.

'A little doll!' sneered Abracadabra. 'There are hundreds of little dolls,' and if Ivy could have heard him through the window she would have said, 'Not for me.'

Ivy gazed at Holly through the window.

She gazed so hard she did not hear footsteps coming down the street, heavy steps and light ones and a queer snuffling sound. The heavy steps were Mr Jones's, the light ones were Peter's, and the snuffling sound was Peter trying not to cry.

'I put it in my pocket,' Peter was saying. 'I forgot my pocket was torn. Oh, what shall I do? What shall I do?' said Peter.

Mr Jones patted his shoulder and asked, 'What sort of key was it now?'

A key? Ivy turned round. She saw Mr Jones and jumped. Then she made herself as small as she could against the window.

'A big iron key, but it looked like silver,' said Peter. He and Mr Jones began to look along the pavement.

It looked like silver. Ivy could feel the edges of the key in her pocket, but – If I go away softly the policeman won't notice me, thought Ivy.

'Mr Blossom trusted me,' said Peter. His wide smile was gone and his face looked quite pale. I don't like boys, thought Ivy, but Peter was saying, 'He trusted me. He'll never trust me again,' and though Peter was a big boy, when he said that he looked as if he really might burst into tears.

A boy cry? asked Ivy. She had never seen Barnabas cry. I didn't know boys could, thought Ivy.

The toys had all wakened again. 'Poor Peter. Poor Peter'; and the whisper ran around:

'Wish. Wish Peter may find the key. Wish.'

'For that careless boy?' said Abracadabra. 'Why, he might have had us all stolen.'

Peter was saying that himself. 'A thief might have picked it up,' he said.

'It w-wasn't a th-thief. It was m-m-me,' said Ivy and put her hand in her pocket and pulled out the key. 'S-so you n-needn't c-c-cry,' said Ivy to Peter.

Can you imagine how Peter's tears disappeared and his smile came back? 'Cry? Who'd cry?' said Peter scornfully, and Ivy thought it better not to say, 'You.'

Mr Jones put the key in the lock, and it fitted. 'I suppose I had better go in,' said Peter, 'and see if everything's all right.'

'Well, I'm going home,' said Mr Jones. 'You know where I live. If anything's wrong, pop in.' It was as he turned to go home that Mr Jones saw Ivy. 'So – there was something green,' said Mr Jones.

Ivy knew how she must look; her coat and

her hair, her socks and her shoes were dusted with flour from the sacks, she had not been able to comb her hair because she had no comb, her face had smears across it from the toffee apple; and, 'I think you are lost,' said Mr Jones.

His voice was so kind that the empty feeling ached in Ivy; it felt so empty that her mouth began to tremble. She could not shut her lips, but, 'I'm n-not l-lost,' said Ivy. 'I'm g-g-going to m-my g-g-g-grandmother.'

'I see,' said Mr Jones. He looked at Ivy again. 'Where does your grandmother live?' asked Mr Jones.

'H-here,' said Ivy.

'Show me,' said Mr Jones and held out his hand.

Ivy took his hand and led him down the street to the Jones's's house. 'This is m-my g-g-grandmother's,' said Ivy.

Mr Jones seemed rather surprised. 'Are you sure?' asked Mr Jones.

'Qu-quite sure,' said Ivy. 'She has m-my b-breakfast ready.'

'Did you say . . . your breakfast?' asked Mr Jones.

'Of course,' said Ivy, 'I-look in at the w-window. There,' she told him. 'Th-there's my Ch-Christmas t-tree.'

Mr Jones thought a moment. Then: 'Perhaps it is your Christmas tree,' he said.

'Sh-shall we kn-knock?' asked Ivy, but, 'You needn't knock,' said Mr Jones. 'You can come in.'

The toys were all in their places when Peter opened the door. 'No thanks to you,' said Abracadabra.

Perhaps Peter heard him, for Peter said, 'Thanks to that little girl.'

I do not know how it was, but Peter had the idea that Ivy was Mr Jones's little girl. 'He was kind to me,' said Peter, 'and so was she.' Peter was very grateful, and, 'What can I do for them?' he asked. Then: 'I know,' said Peter. Mr Blossom had told him to take any toy, and, 'I'll take her a doll,' said Peter. 'I can slip it into their house easy, without saying a word, but – what doll would she like?' asked Peter.

'A bride doll,' said Abracadabra with a gleam of his eyes.

A bride doll was standing in the corner, and Peter went to pick her up, but he must have put his hand on the pin of her price ticket or a wire in the orange-blossom flowers on her dress, for, 'Ow!' said Peter and drew back his hand.

Abracadabra looked at Holly. Holly smiled.

'All little girls like baby dolls,' said Abracadabra. 'Take her a baby doll.'

There was one baby doll left. She was in the window; Peter reached to take her out, but the safety-pin on the baby doll's bib must have been undone, for, 'Ow!' cried Peter and drew back his hand.

'Hsst! T-whoo!' said Abracadabra to Holly. Holly smiled.

It was the same with the primrose bridesmaid.

'Ow!' cried Peter. The same with the rose.

'Ow!' And, 'Here, I'm getting fed up,' said Peter. 'Who's trying this on?' I do not know what made him look at Abracadabra. Abracadabra's eyes gleamed, but in her place just above Abracadabra, Peter saw Holly.

'Why, of course! The little red Christmas doll,' said Peter. 'The very thing!' But as he stepped up to the glass shelf Abracadabra was there.

Peter said that Abracadabra must have toppled, for a toy owl cannot fly, but it seemed for a moment that Abracadabra was right in his face; the green eyes were close, the spread wings, the hooked beak, and the claws. Peter let out a cry and hit Abracadabra, who fell on the floor. 'Out of my way!' cried Peter, and he gave Abracadabra a kick. Then Abracadabra did fly. He went sailing across the shop and landed head down in the rubbish bin.

'Oooh! Aaah!' cried the toys in terror, but Peter sprang after him and shut the lid down tight.

Then he picked up Holly from the shelf in the window and ran pell-mell to the Jones's'.

*

When Mr Jones and Ivy came in Mrs Jones was in the kitchen with a fork in her hand, turning the sausages. Mr Jones told Ivy to wait in the hall.

'Merry Christmas,' said Mr Jones to Mrs Jones and kissed her.

'Merry Christmas,' said Mrs Jones, but she sounded a little sad.

Mr Jones had a present in his pocket for Mrs Jones, a little gold brooch. He took it out, unwrapped it, and pinned it to her dress. 'Oh, how pretty, Albert!' said Mrs Jones, but she still sounded sad.

'I have another Christmas present for you,' said Mr Jones and laughed. 'It has two legs,' said Mr Jones.

'Two legs?' asked Mrs Jones, and Mr Jones laughed again.

'It can walk and talk,' said Mr Jones and laughed still more, and then he brought Ivy in.

When Mrs Jones saw Ivy she did not laugh; for a moment she stood still, then she dropped the fork and knelt down on the floor and put her hands on Ivy's shoulders. 'Oh, Albert!' said Mrs Jones. 'Albert!' She looked at Ivy for a long time and tears came into her eyes and rolled down her cheeks. Ivy, with her glove, wiped the tears away and the emptiness went out of Ivy and never came back.

'Dearie me!' said Mrs Jones, getting to her feet, 'what am I thinking of? You must have a hot bath at once.'

'Breakfast first,' said Mr Jones, and Ivy asked, 'Couldn't I see my Christmas tree?'

Mrs Jones's living room was as bright and clean as it had looked through the window. The fire was warm on Ivy's legs, the table was close to her now, and in the window was the tree – 'With a star on the top,' whispered Ivy.

'But why, oh why,' Mrs Jones was saying to

Mr Jones outside the door, 'why didn't I buy that little doll?'

'And the shops are shut,' whispered Mr Jones. 'We shall have to explain.'

Ivy did not hear them. 'Red candles!' she was whispering. 'Silver crackers! Glass balls . . . !'

'Well, I'll be danged!' said Mr Jones, for, at the foot of the tree, by the parcel of handkerchiefs, stood Holly.

Though Mrs Jones was a little young to be a grandmother, she and Mr Jones adopted Ivy, which means they took her as their own and, of course, Holly as well. Miss Shepherd came to visit them and arrange this. 'Please tell

Barnabas,' said Ivy.

Mrs Jones made Ivy a green dress like Holly's red one but with a red petticoat and red socks. She made Holly a red coat like Ivy's green one and knitted her a pair of tiny green woollen gloves so that they matched when they went out.

They pass the toyshop often, but there is no Abracadabra.

'Where is the owl?' Mr Blossom had asked when the shop opened again, and Peter had to say, 'I put him in the rubbish bin.'

'Good gracious me!' said Mr Blossom. 'Get him out at once,' but when they lifted the lid Abracadabra was not there.

'Sir, the dustman must have taken him away,' said Peter, standing up stiff and straight. I do not know if that was true, but Abracadabra was never seen again.

'Never seen again,' said the toys. They sounded happy. 'Never seen again,' and long, long afterward in the toyshop they told tales of Abracadabra.

Sometimes Holly and Ivy meet Crumple, who waves his trunk at them. Once they saw

Mallow and Wallow put out on a windowsill. They often see Peter and Mr Blossom; in spite of Abracadabra's disappearance, Mr Blossom trusts Peter.

'But if you had not found the key,' says Peter to Ivy.

'If I had not come to look at Holly,' says Ivy.

'If I had not gone to Mr Jones,' says Peter.

'If Mrs Jones had not bought the Christmas tree' – but it goes further back than that. If Ivy had not slept in the shed . . . If the baker had not lit his oven . . . If Ivy had not got out of the train . . . If Barnabas had not laughed at Ivy . . . If Holly . . .

'If I had not wished,' says Holly.

I told you it was a story about wishing.